MW01252291

MOTORCYCLE GEAR

MOTORCYCLE MANIA

David and Patricia Armentrout

Rourke
Publishing LLC
Vero Beach, Florida 32964

www.rourkepublishing.com

PHOTO CREDITS: Cover and pp. 8, 11 ©Daniel Gustavsson; pp. 4 ©afaizal; pp. 6 ©Tan Kian Khoon ; pp. 7, 22 ©Brad Angus; pp. 9 ©zimmytws; pp. 10 ©Graham Prentice; pp. 12 ©Pascal Janssen; pp. 13 ©Robert Kelsey; pp. 14 ©Mark Yuill; pp. 15 ©Sean Nel; pp. 16 ©Roberto Aquilano; pp. 17 ©Drue T. Overby; pp. 18, 20 ©Honda; pp. 19 ©Linda Muir; pp. 21 ©Yamaha.

Title page: *Leather saddlebags are popular motorcycle gear.*

Editor: Robert Stengard-Olliges

Cover design by Nicola Stratford

Library of Congress Cataloging-in-Publication Data

Armentrout, David, 1962-
Motorcycle gear / David and Patricia Armentrout.
p. cm. -- (Motorcycle mania II)
ISBN-13: 978-1-60044-588-0
1. Motorcycles--Juvenile literature. 2. Motorcycling--Juvenile literature. I. Armentrout, Patricia, 1960- II. Title.
TL440.15.A757 2008
629.28'475--dc22
2007016377

Printed in the USA

CG/CG

Rourke Publishing

www.rourkepublishing.com – rourke@rourkepublishing.com
Post Office Box 3328, Vero Beach, FL 32964

TABLE OF CONTENTS

CYCLE GEAR

There are motorcycles designed for high-speed racing, and some for long distance touring. Some motorcycles are meant for paved surfaces and others for rough off-road trails. It's no surprise then, that cycle gear, equipment, and accessories are also designed for every kind of motorcycle and for every riding style.

Motorcycle racers wear tight-fitting, protective leather suits.

agv
KERAKOLL
MOTUL
KERAKOLL
FASTWEB
IMATRA
R.C., INC
YAMAHA
YAMAHA
CAMEL
CAMEL
YAMAHA
YAMAHA
DOCTOR
YAMAHA
YAMAHA
CAMEL

SAFETY FIRST

To many, motorcycling is more than a form of transportation; it's a fun motor sport. But riding on two wheels is riskier than on four. That's why safety gear is a must.

Riders maneuver to avoid an unlucky racer.

The helmet is the most important piece of safety gear. It protects the head during impact, reducing injuries and deaths.

A helmet, gloves, and ear plugs protect riders.

HEADS UP

Full face helmets provide the best protection. They cover the entire skull and chin and have a protective face shield. Open face helmets cover the skull but don't offer chin protection. A half helmet, also called a shorty, doesn't cover or protect the lower rear part of the skull. Half helmets also come off easier upon impact.

Goggles protect enduro riders from flying dirt and mud.

This shorty helmet has a nice design but it doesn't provide the best protection.

Bikers usually wear a clear or tinted face shield, goggles, or wraparound sunglasses when riding.

LEATHERS

Leathers are the clothes worn by motorcyclists. Leathers fit tight so they can't get caught on anything. Black leather jackets and pants are traditional pieces worn by bikers. And while the biker look is popular, leathers are really about safety. Riding gear is constructed from heavy weight leather that protects against skin abrasions and puncture wounds resulting from a fall.

A touring motorcyclist is dressed from head to toe in protective gear.

Experienced riders know how important protective gear is.

Motorcyclists who race wear full body suits made of leather or **Kevlar**. Racing leathers have extra foam padding and hard plastic **armor** in the shoulders, spine, elbows, and knees. No racer would want to take a spill without body armor.

Racing leathers combine natural leather, synthetic fabrics, and hard plastic armor.

A motocross racer wears extra armor on his chest and shoulders.

GLOVES AND BOOTS

Leather gloves and boots provide comfort and protection. Boots should cover the ankles, and have slip resistant soles with heels that grip the bike's footpegs.

Gloves offer protection and improve grip.

Leather boots protect the foot and ankle, while hard plastic "sliders" protect the knees.

There are a variety of racing boots to choose from. **Motocross** boots have protective armor above the ankle. Sport bike racing boots have extra protection around the toe and heel. **Speedway** racers wear a metal plate on their left boot. The plate keeps the boot from wearing away as riders drag their foot into the turns.

JUST FOR BIKES

Motorcyclists equip their bikes with safety gear, too. **Fairings**, like **aerodynamic** panels and windshields, protect riders from wind, airborne debris, and rain. They are common on sport and touring bikes. Fairings are sold as aftermarket parts too, so they can be added to bikes that don't have them.

Italian Highway Police motorcycles have windshields, body panels, and rear luggage compartments.

Body panels that cover the engine are called cowlings.

Most racers use a trailer to transport their bikes. A bike stand, tools, and spare bike parts also come in handy.

LUGGAGE

The biker term for motorcycle storage is luggage. Some bikes have built-in hard luggage mounted on each side of the rear wheel. Motorcycles can also be fitted with luggage racks and soft luggage, including tank bags, seat or saddlebags, and tail packs. Luggage is great for storing helmets, rain gear, and bike covers when they're not in use.

Leather saddlebags are stylish and functional.

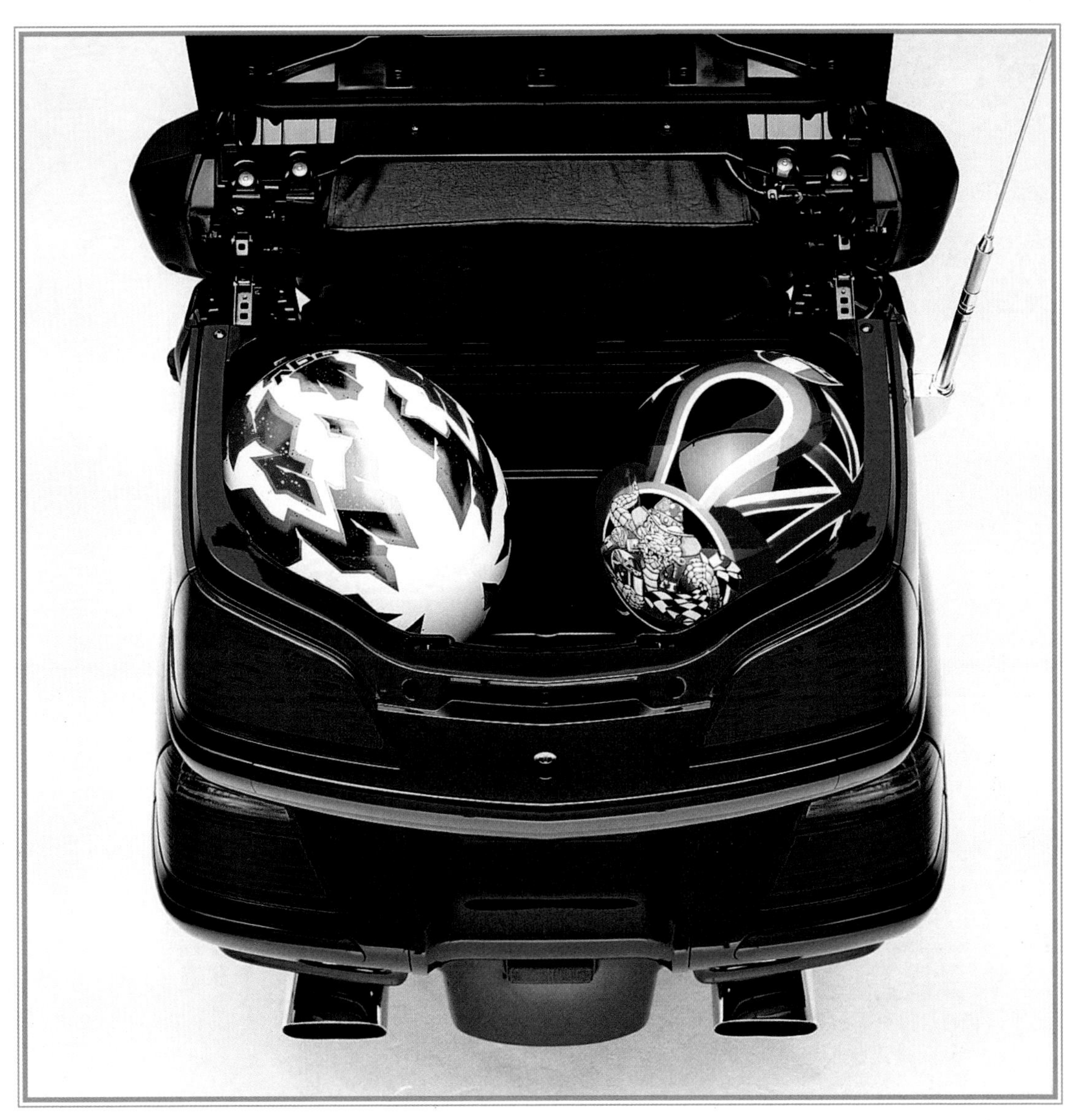

A large rear luggage compartment can hold two helmets and has a little extra space.

Horns, mirrors, foot pegs, gas caps, seats, sissy bars, and crash bars can be added or changed on most motorcycles. Accessories like these really personalize a bike.

GRIPPING THE ROAD

The helmet may be the rider's most important piece of safety gear, but the tires will make or break the bike. The right motorcycle tires provide the best handling and the safest ride.

MOTORCYCLE TYPE	TIRE NEEDS
Cruiser	hard rubber, various tread patterns *operate well at all temperature cycles*
Touring bike	hard rubber with treads *stable, long lasting, all season*
Racer	soft rubber *get hot and sticky from use, grip well*
Dragster	soft rubber *get hot and sticky from use, grip well*
Trail/Dirt bike	knobby tires, deep treads *best for loose soil, sand, mud, and gravel*

Racing bikes have soft rubber tires that heat up, get sticky, and really grip the road.

Knobby tires get good traction in loose soil.

Did you know the section of tire that touches the road surface is called the contact patch?

SPECIAL EQUIPMENT

Some motorcycle sports require special equipment, such as tire warmers and wheelie bars. Tire warmers, used in sport bike racing, warm tires up before a race. A wheelie bar, attached to the rear of a drag bike, helps keep the front wheel on the pavement during a fast and hard acceleration.

There are lots of ways to have fun on a motorcycle, whether its drag racing, dirt riding, or just cruising the countryside. But doing it with the right gear and equipment is the best and safest way.

Tire warmers bring racing tires up to temperature before a race.

GLOSSARY

aerodynamic (air oh dye NAM ik) — designed to move through the air easily and quickly

armor (ARE mer) — protective coverings

fairings (FAIR ingz) — devices such as windshields and body panels that are mounted on the front of a motorcycle to protect the rider from windblast

Kevlar (KEV lar) — a brand name for a very strong, but lightweight man-made fabric

motocross (MOE toe kross) — cross-country motorcycle racing

speedway (SPEED way) — a form of dirt track motorcycle racing

INDEX

FURTHER READING

Schuette, Sarah L. *Harley-Davidson Motorcycles.* Capstone Press, 2006.
Mezzanotte, Jim. *Hillclimb.* Gareth Stevens Audio, 2006.
Norman, Tony. *Motorcycle Racing*. Gareth Stevens Audio, 2006.

WEBSITES TO VISIT

www.amadirectlink.com
www.msf-usa.org

ABOUT THE AUTHORS

David and Patricia Armentrout specialize in writing nonfiction books for young readers. They have had several books published for primary school reading. The Armentrouts live in Cincinnati, Ohio, with their two children.